The Bride of Frankenstein Doesn't Bake Cookies

by **Debbie Dadey**
and
Marcia Thornton Jones

illustrated by **John Steven Gurney**

A
LITTLE APPLE
PAPERBACK

SCHOLASTIC INC.
New York   Toronto   London   Auckland   Sydney
Mexico City   New Delhi   Hong Kong

To Mrs. Kaminski's winning students in
Springvale, Maine! — MTJ and DD

ISBN 0-439-04400-6

Text copyright © 2000 by Marcia Thornton Jones and Debra S. Dadey.
Illustrations copyright © 2000 by Scholastic Inc.
SCHOLASTIC, LITTLE APPLE PAPERBACKS, THE ADVENTURES OF THE BAILEY
SCHOOL KIDS, and associated logos are trademarks of Scholastic Inc.

12 11 10 9 8 7 6 5 4 3 2 1   0 1 2 3 4 5/0

Printed in the U.S.A.   40

First Scholastic printing, May 2000

Contents

1

Sad Monster

"Something's wrong with Frank," Eddie told his friends Melody and Howie.

The three kids stared at the huge man standing at the Bailey City Ice Skating Complex's brand-new snack bar. Even though he was slumped over, his head still nearly touched the bright purple sign hanging over the snack bar. The neon glow lit up his pale face and made the jagged scar on his cheek look even bigger.

"Of course something's wrong with Frank," Melody agreed. "After all, he looks just like the Frankenstein monster. That's enough to depress anybody. Come on, let's get some hot chocolate and sugar cookies."

Five minutes later the kids sat at one of the purple tables in the snack area. Through a big glass window they watched their friend Liza whiz past them during her ice-skating lesson. Behind them they heard Frank groan, "Hrrmm." The kids turned in time to see Frank drop his head into his giant hands. His sigh was so big it blew a stack of napkins off the counter.

"He looks like he lost his best friend," Howie said softly, hoping Frank wouldn't overhear.

"I hope not," Melody whispered, "because Dr. Victor is Frank's *only* friend." Dr. Victor was the curator of the Shelley Museum. Once, the kids had gone to the museum on a third-grade field trip. After getting lost in the museum, they found Dr. Victor's secret laboratory. To the kids it looked exactly like a monster-making laboratory.

Howie wiped hot chocolate off his mouth. "He's not just a friend," Howie added. "Dr. Victor is the scientist who made Frank."

"We don't know that Frank is really a Frankenstein monster," Eddie pointed out while tossing his red baseball cap onto the table. "Maybe he's just a really big athlete."

"Shhh. It's still not a good idea to make him mad," Howie told him. "Remember what happened when Frank and Dr. Victor got into a fight?"

Melody and Eddie nodded. Frank left his job at the Shelley Museum to be a hockey coach after having a fight with Dr. Victor. The kids worried that Frank would take over Bailey City until he finally made up with Dr. Victor. "It's not smart to make a monster mad," Melody agreed.

"Maybe Frank is only sad that these cookies are so small," Eddie griped after he'd wolfed down five of the tiny sugar cookies. "This snack bar will never make any money serving shrimpy little cookies like these."

"I don't think Frank is worrying about cookies," Howie said.

"We're about to find out," Melody said, "because Dr. Victor just walked through the door!"

2

Mad Scientist

Melody stared at Frank. He was hunched over with his head on the snack bar counter and did not see Dr. Victor walk in. Every once in a while Frank groaned and slowly bumped his head on the counter.

"That has to hurt," Melody said as Frank hit his forehead on the counter.

Eddie shook his head. "Frank's head is made of steel — nothing could hurt it except a cruise missile."

"Actually, I think a friend could hurt Frank," Howie said softly. "I think Frank is a lot more sensitive than we think."

Melody shrugged. "I guess even a monster has feelings. I hope Dr. Victor isn't going to make him feel worse." The kids watched Dr. Victor make his way around the ice-skating rink.

"If you ask me, Dr. Victor looks worried," Howie said.

"I'd be worried, too," Eddie joked, "if my only friend was a monster."

"Shh," Melody hissed. "Here he comes."

Dr. Victor rushed past the kids and sat next to Frank. Dr. Victor put his hand on Frank's shoulder and the two talked quietly.

"I'd pay five bucks to hear what they're saying," Eddie said.

"If you *had* five bucks," Melody said.

Eddie threw cookie crumbs at Melody. "I have ten dollars saved from my birthday money. I've been saving it for something special."

Melody rolled her eyes. "That's practically a miracle." Eddie always spent his money as quickly as he got it. He was usually weeks behind in his allowance.

"This isn't good," Howie whispered.

Melody was surprised. "Saving money is a good thing," she said.

Howie put his finger to his lips. "I'm

7

not talking about Eddie's birthday money. I'm talking about Frank and Dr. Victor." The kids sipped hot chocolate and stared at the two men. It was obvious they disagreed about something. Both of them frowned and Dr. Victor started pounding the counter with his fist.

Suddenly, Dr. Victor shouted, "*No!* I will not do it. I vowed never to mix that recipe again!"

Frank put his head down on the counter. "Hrrrmm!" he groaned.

"Is he crying?" Melody asked softly.

Howie shrugged as Dr. Victor lowered his voice to whisper something to Frank. Finally Dr. Victor stood up. He was pale and shaking. "You have forced my hand," he told Frank. "I will do what you ask," he added in a trembling voice. "But I am not responsible for what happens!"

Then Dr. Victor rushed from the rink, leaving a cold chill behind him in the snack bar.

3

Monster's Girlfriend

"You should have heard Dr. Victor," Melody told Liza as the kids walked home from the skating rink. "He sounded as if he were planning the end of the world."

Eddie rolled his eyes. "Don't be crazy. He was probably just telling Frank he'd do his laundry for him."

"I wish dirty socks were all that Dr. Victor had in mind," Howie said, looking back over his shoulder at the Bailey City Ice Skating Complex. "I think Dr. Victor and Frank are devising a terrible plan."

Liza shook her blond head. "They were probably only talking about cookie recipes."

Howie stared at Liza. "Don't you remember?" Howie said. "You were the one who was sure Frank was really the Frankenstein monster."

"That's right," Melody said to Liza. "You thought Dr. Victor cooked up Frank using his secret formula Big."

Liza's face turned red. "Yeah, but I also remember how sad Frank was when he didn't have any friends. Everyone should have a friend."

"He has Dr. Victor for a friend," Howie reminded her.

Liza nodded. "I think he needs more friends. He still seems lonely. Maybe we should be more friendly."

"It sounds like you want to be a monster's girlfriend," Eddie teased.

Liza stopped walking down the sidewalk and put her hands on her hips. "You listen to me," she told Eddie. "It doesn't matter what a person looks like, it's what's on the inside that counts. After all, sometimes you *act* like a monster, but we're still *your* friends!"

Thick clouds rolled over Bailey City as

they walked without saying another word. Thunder rumbled closer and closer. Wind blew small tree branches across the sidewalk. The four friends hurried to make it to Eddie's house before the rain started.

Eddie opened the back door. "Hurry," he said. "It's going to pour any minute."

Howie paused and pointed toward a huge streak of lightning in the distance. "Isn't that where the Shelley Museum is?" he asked.

The kids watched as more lightning stretched toward the distant museum. Thunder boomed so loudly the windows rattled and the ground shook. "That was loud enough to wake the dead," Eddie said with a laugh.

"I have a feeling this storm is nothing to joke about," Howie said hoarsely. But his three friends had already gone inside to the safety of the kitchen and his words were lost in the thunder.

4

Monster Cookies

Liza tapped her watch and frowned at Eddie as he jogged across the Bailey School playground. "Hurry!" she yelled. "I'm going to be late for my skating lesson."

It had been a week since the kids saw Frank and Dr. Victor arguing at the skating rink. Liza, Melody, and Howie waited under the oak tree as Eddie ran up to them.

"Don't get your tutu in a bunch," Eddie told her as he stopped to tie a shoelace. "The ice won't melt if you're a few minutes late."

"If I miss something good," Liza told him, "you'll be sorry!"

"Eddie is never sorry," Melody told Liza. "But I wonder if Frank is still sad."

"I'm sure Frank is just hunky-dory," Eddie told her as the four friends headed toward the rink.

"I just can't get that storm out of my mind," Howie said.

Liza nodded. "I don't like storms, either," she said. "But we have nothing to worry about. The sun is shining and there isn't a cloud in the sky!"

"I wasn't worried about the storm," Howie told her. "I was worried about the museum. And Dr. Victor."

"I'm sure everything is fine," Melody told Howie as they neared the skating rink.

"I hope so," Howie said, "but I have a very strange feeling about that lightning over the Shelley Museum."

"I have a very strange feeling, too," Eddie said as he rubbed his stomach. "Hunger! My stomach is so empty I could eat five dozen cookies!"

"Five dozen would be the same as sixty

cookies," Liza told Eddie. "Not even you could eat that many."

"Those cookies at the skating rink are so tiny, I bet I could eat three times that many!" Eddie bragged as he pulled open the door to the rink. "I'll prove it as soon as we get to the snack bar!"

But Eddie couldn't prove anything. In fact, the four friends couldn't even get into the snack bar because there were so many people lined up to buy cookies.

"What is going on?" Liza asked. "I've never seen this many people crowded into the skating rink."

Eddie hopped up on a table to get a good look at what was happening. Melody, Liza, and Howie each stood on a chair.

"Who is that?" Liza asked over the noise of the crowd. There were at least a hundred people in line to get cookies, but Melody, Howie, and Eddie knew just who Liza was talking about.

A strange woman stood behind the

cookie counter. She was taller than everybody else. Everyone, that is, except Frank. Frank towered over the entire crowd as he watched the stranger take orders. Dr. Victor stood by Frank's elbow.

"It looks like her hair is full of electricity," Eddie said. The lady's hair stuck straight up and was as black as a coffin except for two white streaks above her ears.

"Shh," Liza warned. "She'll hear you. That hairstyle is called a beehive."

"I know why," Eddie said with a laugh. "There are enough tangles in her hair to hide a beehive and a nest of spiders for a year."

Melody shook her head. "We'd see them crawling over the white streaks," she pointed out.

"It looks like you'll have to wait to eat your cookies," Liza told Eddie. "The line is getting even longer."

"I don't get it," Eddie said. "The cookies aren't that good."

"There's only one way to find out," Howie said. "We have to get closer."

Liza shook her head. "If we stand in that line, I'll definitely be late for my skating class."

"I'm not talking about standing in line," Howie said. "I'm thinking about a sneak peek at those cookies."

"Now you're talking," Eddie said. "And I'm the professional sneak in this group. Follow me!"

The three friends followed Eddie as he

darted between tables, pushed past a crowd of people, and crawled between the legs of a man who wouldn't let them by. Finally they stood at the end of the counter.

The strange lady's cookies were huge. So huge it took two hands to hold them. "Those aren't the same cookies that were here last week," Howie said.

Eddie whistled and Liza licked her lips. Melody giggled. "I'd like to see Eddie eat five dozen of *those* cookies," she said.

"It looks like that lady found out about Dr. Victor's secret formula Big," Liza whispered.

"It's worse than that," Howie said. He turned to explain what he meant, but when he did, he saw something that turned his face as pale as the ice in the rink. Dr. Victor was heading straight for them.

"I see you have noticed the . . . er . . . changes at the snack counter," Dr. Victor said.

"Who wouldn't notice monster cookies like that!" Eddie said. "I can't wait to taste one!"

"Then you shall," Dr. Victor said with a smile. "After all, you are my best customers. Please, follow me."

Dr. Victor brought Eddie, Melody, Liza, and Howie to the front of the line. Frank followed close behind.

"I would like you to meet . . . um . . . my niece Electra," Dr. Victor told them.

"She . . . er . . . arrived last week." Electra wore a long white skirt that swept across the floor as she turned to face Dr. Victor, Frank, and the four kids. Electra acted like her neck was sore. She held her head stiffly and walked like all her joints needed oil.

"Electra, I would like you to meet Liza, Eddie, Howie, and Melody," Dr. Victor said to the lady. "They came to try your cookies."

She gave each kid a jerky nod. "So very nice to meet you," she said. "My goal is to have the most successful cookie counter in the country." Electra spoke like she moved, in funny little jerks.

Then Electra turned to Frank and smiled. That's when Howie saw something that made him gulp.

Frank blushed!

5

Monster Disgrace

The four friends settled into a booth close to the counter to eat their monster cookies, but Howie didn't bite into his right away.

"What's wrong with you?" Eddie said with his mouth full of peanut butter cookie.

"Are you sick?" Melody asked.

"I get his cookie if he's sick," Eddie said and reached across the table for Howie's chocolate chip cookie.

Howie pulled his snack out of Eddie's reach. "I'm not sick. But I just saw something that gave me a case of the shivers," he told his friends.

"We're in an ice rink," Eddie told Howie. "It's supposed to be cold."

"Not that kind of shivers," Howie said.

"I'm talking about goose bumps. I think Frank likes the new cookie chef."

"So?" Melody asked. "She's very nice."

Liza nodded. "I like her."

"Me too," Eddie said. "She makes a mean cookie."

"I'm not talking about *like*," Howie tried to explain. "I mean he LIKES her, *really* likes her."

Melody smiled. "That's so sweet."

"I think it's sick," Eddie said.

The four friends glanced at the snack counter. Electra's new monster cookies were selling like crazy. She was so busy, Frank stepped up to help fill mugs with steaming hot chocolate and Dr. Victor hurried to put more cookies in the oven. But still, the line grew longer and longer.

"Your suggestion was wonderful," the kids heard Electra tell Frank. "Bigger cookies mean bigger sales! I have you to thank!"

Electra was so excited she stopped

long enough to give Frank a big smooch on the cheek.

Frank looked down at his huge shoes. He blushed. He giggled. Then he covered his face and hurried from the snack bar. The hot chocolate in Howie's mug splashed with each step Frank took.

"Isn't that cute?" Liza said with a sigh. "I think Frank is in *love!*"

"It's disgusting," Eddie said. "Frank is a disgrace to all of monsterdom!"

"Electra looks a little bit like a monster herself," Melody said. "So maybe it's okay."

"Then you know it, too?" Howie gasped.

"Know what?" Liza asked.

Howie pulled Melody, Liza, and Eddie close to him so nobody could overhear what he had to say.

"Electra isn't really Dr. Victor's niece, and she's not a cookie chef," Howie whispered. "She's a monster just like Frank.

In fact, I believe Dr. Victor created Electra to be Frank's friend. His girlfriend!"

Eddie spat out a bite of cookie. "That's the most ridiculous thing you've ever said," Eddie told his friend. "Monsters and l-o-v-e don't mix." He spelled the word so he wouldn't have to say it.

Liza nodded. "The only monster we need to worry about is Howie's giant imagination."

Melody shrugged. "I'm not sure if I believe in monsters or not, but I'm sure we have nothing to worry about. In fact," she told them, "if Electra really is another Frankenstein monster, our monster problems will be over for good. All we have to do is get Frank married off to Electra and he's history."

"You make it sound like you die after you get married," Howie said.

"Marriage sounds worse than death if you ask me," Eddie said matter-of-factly.

"A monster marriage could be bad for Bailey City," Howie warned them. "If Electra really is the Bride of Frankenstein then we could have little baby monsters taking over Bailey City!"

"What's wrong with that?" Eddie asked before swiping a bite from Howie's uneaten cookie.

"For one thing, nobody will pay any attention to *you* with monsters running loose everywhere," Howie pointed out.

Eddie pounded the table. "That does it. Howie is right. This gooey monster-romance horror must be stopped!"

6

Monster Trouble

"We have nothing to worry about," Melody said, trying to calm Eddie down. "I'm sure the Bride of Frankenstein doesn't bake cookies. We don't even know if Frank really likes Electra."

"What's not to like? Electra's beautiful in a monster kind of way. She's smart, and she makes a great cookie," Liza said.

Eddie groaned. "This lovey-dovey talk is making me sick."

"Liza's right about Electra," Howie said, "and I think Frank has noticed, too."

The kids looked out at the ice where Howie pointed. Frank wore ice skates and had changed into his Thunderbolts hockey uniform. He used a hockey stick to sweep a puck to a spot right in front of the snack bar.

29

As soon as Frank was sure Electra was watching, he zipped around the rink so fast he became a giant blur.

"Wow!" Eddie said. "Frank can really move. But why is he skating so fast? Nobody's chasing him."

"Because," Melody said with a smile, "he wants Electra to see what a good skater he is."

"Why?" Eddie asked.

Liza rolled her eyes. "Don't you know anything about flirting?" she asked. "Frank is showing off just for Electra because he *likes* her."

"Yuck," Eddie said. His faced turned a pale shade of green and he put his fingers in his ears so he couldn't hear another word. "I don't know anything about flirting, and I don't want to learn!"

Electra didn't seem to care, either. She turned away from the rink to pull another batch of cookies out of the oven.

"Uh-oh," Howie said. "This could be very dangerous."

"What's dangerous about a hockey player showing off for a girl?" Liza asked.

"It's dangerous when that hockey player is a monster in love," Howie warned. "Frank won't stop until Electra notices him. That could only mean one thing. Trouble. Monster trouble."

It looked like Howie might be right. Frank waited until Electra glanced his way again, and then he cut through the center of the rink. He did three figure eights before slamming his hockey puck into the goal.

Frank looked at the cookie counter to see if Electra had seen him.

Electra wasn't even watching. She was too busy serving cookies to all her customers to notice Frank.

"Hhhhrrrrm!" Frank roared. Then he pushed off with his skate, building up to a speed faster than anybody had ever skated. He leaped into the air and spun like a tornado out of control.

Unfortunately, Frank was going too fast. He landed on the ice. Hard. His skates slipped out from under him and he fell down. The ice cracked when he landed.

Everybody gasped. They held their breath. Frank had everybody's attention now. Even Electra's.

The entire ice-skating rink was silent for a full minute. Then the silence was broken by a terrible sound. Electra was laughing! Soon, everybody giggled along with her.

"HHHHRRRRM!" Frank roared. His face turned pink. Then it turned red. The scar on his cheek turned a deep shade of purple. Frank scrambled up from the ice and slammed the hockey puck so hard it cracked a board into pieces.

7

Nightmares for Life

"Frank will get over being embarrassed," Melody said. "We don't have to worry."

Liza, Howie, Eddie, and Melody had just left the rink after Liza's skating lesson.

"I'm not so sure," Liza said sadly. "Getting laughed at by the girl you love is pretty bad."

"Frank is not in l-o-v-e," Eddie said. "He was only practicing new skating moves. Now, will you stop talking about this romance stuff before you give me nightmares for life?"

Howie patted Eddie on the shoulder. "Maybe you're right," Howie said. "After Frank fell he disappeared from the rink."

"That's right," Eddie said. "If he really was a monster in l-o-v-e then he would have terrorized us all day long."

"Maybe Eddie is right," Melody said.

"Whew," Eddie sighed with relief. "You had me worried. I'm glad this monster l-o-v-e is dead and buried. Let's celebrate with a Doodlegum Shake!"

Melody, Liza, and Howie followed Eddie to Burger Doodle Restaurant. Just as Eddie reached for the door, Liza grabbed his arm.

"We can't go in there," she warned. "Look!"

The kids peered through the window. What they saw made Eddie groan. Electra sat in a corner booth. And she wasn't alone. A tall man in a gray suit sat across from her. They both laughed as if they'd just heard one of Eddie's jokes.

"Poor Frank," Melody said. "Electra must not like him at all."

Liza nodded. "It looks like she already has a boyfriend."

36

Howie moaned. He groaned. Then Howie sat down on the ground.

"What's wrong?" Liza asked.

"Somebody call a doctor!" Melody screamed.

But Howie reached out and stopped them before anyone ran for the phone. "There's only one doctor who can help cure this Bailey City monster menace," Howie said. "Dr. Victor!"

"What are you talking about?" Eddie asked. "I thought we were going to forget all that monster mush."

Howie sighed and put his head in his hands. His three friends sat on the ground around Howie so they could hear him.

"I just remembered what happened to the real Frankenstein monster when a bride was created for him," Howie said, his voice shaking at the memory. "Like Electra, the Bride of Frankenstein didn't love the Monster. The Monster was so devastated, he destroyed everything. We can't let that happen to Bailey City!"

"But you're talking about a movie," Melody said. "This is real life."

Howie nodded. "That's exactly why it's so important that we make sure Electra likes Frank," he explained.

Eddie scratched his head. "I thought you didn't want Frank and Electra to get married," he said, "because then there'd be lots of little monsters taking over Bailey City."

"That was before I realized how dangerous our situation was," Howie told them.

Melody nodded. "I think I understand," she said. "Frank must be happy. After all, an unhappy monster terrorizing Bailey City could mean the end of us all!"

8

Monster at the Mall

"This is the life," Eddie said. "Saturday night and a movie at the mall."

Liza moved in line behind Eddie at the ticket booth. "It was nice of your grandmother to bring us to the mall."

"She loves the mall," Eddie said. "She can shop while we're inside the theater."

"Oh my gosh," Melody squealed. "There's Electra!" The kids turned to see Electra dressed in a bright blue shiny dress. She was laughing with a man. It was the same man the kids had seen at Burger Doodle.

"I didn't know they let monsters come to the mall," Eddie joked.

"This isn't funny," Melody said. "Electra is on a date with someone else! What

if she marries that man instead of Frank? Frank will destroy Bailey City!"

Liza put her hand on Melody's shoulder. "Just because people are on a date doesn't mean that they're going to get married. People should know each other for a long time before they get married."

But Melody didn't agree. "We have to stop them before this gets serious."

"I know what we can do," Liza said. "We'll convince Electra that Frank likes her better than that stranger does." Liza and Melody left the ticket booth and rushed over to Electra.

"What about my popcorn and movie?" Eddie complained.

Howie grabbed Eddie and pulled him toward Electra. "There are some things more important than your stomach," Howie told his friend.

By the time the boys caught up, Liza was already telling Electra that Frank thought she was the best cook in the entire world. "That's why there's always such a long line at the snack bar," Liza said.

"That's right," Melody joined in. "Frank thinks everyone would love to buy your cookies. You should sell them everywhere."

Electra blushed as Howie said, "Thanks to your monster cookies, business is booming at the snack bar."

The tall man in the gray suit smiled at Electra. "I agree with you kids. Electra is a *huge* success."

Electra smiled at the man and batted her long eyelashes as the two of them walked away.

The four kids groaned as they watched Electra and the man sit down at a nearby table. They leaned their heads close together in a serious conversation.

"All we did was make the strange man like Electra more," Melody groaned.

"I think our monster problem just turned into a nightmare!" Howie said with a gulp.

9

Real Life

"That was a great movie," Eddie said as he swung on a branch of the oak tree. Eddie, Melody, Howie, and Liza were all under the tree. It was their meeting place before school. "Of course, it would have been better if it had more monsters in it," Eddie added.

Liza twirled around under the tree, letting her blond ponytail fly out behind her. "I liked the part where the kid swings into the garbage like Tarzan."

Melody laughed. "It was funny when he came up with a banana on his head."

"I still think the book was better," Howie said, dropping his Bailey School backpack onto the ground.

Eddie rolled his eyes. "Real life is better than books any day."

"Movies aren't real life," Howie told Eddie.

Before Howie and Eddie got into a fight, Liza interrupted. "Speaking of real life, I realized I did something wrong at the mall. Instead of telling Electra that Frank likes her, we have to make Electra like Frank."

"Why would we want to do that?" Eddie asked.

"Because it's a nice thing to do," Liza said.

"The only person I plan to help is me," Eddie bragged. "I want to help myself to some more of those giant cookies. Besides," he added, "I thought you were afraid of little monsters running all over Bailey City."

"I thought about that, too," Liza said. "And I realized that Frank would never want to have kids after hanging around with you."

Eddie stopped swinging on the tree limb and jumped down in front of Liza.

"Very funny, banana brains, but there's no reason for us to help Frank," Eddie said.

"Yes, there is," Melody said. "After all, he helped us start the new Junior Thunderbolts hockey team." The kids nodded and remembered how much fun they'd had learning about hockey.

"He taught us how to work together as a team," Howie added.

"And he gave us giant petunias when we visited the Shelley Museum," Liza added.

"The girls are right," Howie said. "Frank has always been our friend."

"Besides, we have to save Bailey City. If Frank thinks Electra hates him, there's no telling what could happen," Liza said. "And I know just what to do."

10

Smithereens

"Follow me," Liza told her friends. "I have the perfect plan for getting Electra to like Frank."

Without waiting for her friends to answer, Liza took off running down the street. Her friends had to hurry to catch up.

Electra was busy behind the cookie counter when the kids got to the rink. She opened the huge oven and slid out a tray of golden cookies. Then she slid in another tray before facing the long line of customers. She was so busy she didn't even see Frank, but the kids did.

Frank hid in the shadows at the end of the counter. He didn't stand tall and straight like he normally did. Instead,

Frank's shoulders were slumped and his head hung low.

"Hhhhrrrrm," Frank groaned, but Electra didn't hear him over the noise of the crowd.

"Poor Frank," Liza said. "I've never seen him so sad."

"He looks like he's getting even worse," Melody warned.

"HHHHRRRRM," Frank growled from the shadows as more people joined the line for Electra's cookies. Nobody noticed Frank. They were only interested in cookies.

"Frank should be glad the counter is packed," Eddie pointed out to his friends. "Think of all the dough he's making — and I'm not talking about cookie dough!"

"Some things are more important than money," Liza told Eddie. "Like love."

"Ewww, yuck!" Eddie sputtered. "All this gooey talk has turned your brains to mush."

"I'm not worried about our brains turning to mush," Howie told Eddie. "We need to worry about all of Bailey City being kicked to smithereens by a very hurt monster!"

"Electra needs more time to get to know Frank," Liza said quickly. "Then she'll see how nice he is."

"How can she do that?" Melody asked. "There are too many people here. Electra doesn't even have time to take a breath."

"Then we have to get rid of all these customers," Liza said. "It's the only way."

"That sounds like fun," Eddie said with a grin. "Leave the customers to me."

"I thought you didn't believe in monster love," Liza asked Eddie.

Eddie shook his head. "There's only one kind of l-o-v-e I believe in, and that's for cookies. As soon as all these people are out of the way then I can be first in line!"

Before anybody could argue with him, Eddie rushed across the snack bar to get in line.

"Eddie never stands in a line," Liza said. "We better get over there and see what he's up to."

"Coach O'Grady told us eating right is a key ingredient to being a winning athlete," Eddie was telling two teenagers dressed in hockey gear when his friends joined the line. "He said not to eat junk food like cookies. But I guess you don't *really* want to be good hockey players."

The two teenagers looked at each other. "The kid's right," one of them said. "We shouldn't eat cookies if we want to be athletes." Then the teenagers left the snack bar.

Eddie moved up in line. He tugged on the sweater sleeve of a mother with her three kids. Eddie batted his eyelashes and smiled so she could see all of his teeth. "I just got back from seeing my dentist. Dr. Herb says things with sugar are bad for teeth. Do cookies have sugar in them?"

The young mother looked at the giant cookies. Then she looked at her kids. "You're right," she told Eddie. "We shouldn't eat all that sugar."

Eddie moved up in line when the woman pulled her three screaming kids from the snack bar. Eddie cleared his throat and the four grandmothers standing in front of him turned around.

"I wonder if you know my grandmother," Eddie said politely. "She just lost fifty pounds. Nurse Redding told my grandmother to follow the food pyramid if she didn't want to be fat. Cookies aren't on the food pyramid, are they?"

The grandmothers turned red. "I've decided I don't want a cookie after all," one lady said to another.

Eddie grinned and moved up in line. When Eddie got up to the counter Electra smiled and gave him a cookie. Then she looked behind Eddie. "What happened to all my customers?" she gasped. "They've disappeared!"

Electra looked out at the empty snack bar. The smile faded from her face. One tear trickled down her cheek.

Melody rushed over to Frank. "Quick," she told him. "You have to cheer up Electra!"

Frank stood up straight. He smiled a lopsided grin and nodded. "Must cheer up Electra," Frank repeated.

Frank stepped behind the counter and batted his eyelashes. He blushed when Electra smiled at him.

"Whew," Liza said. "I think it's working."

Liza was right. Electra and Frank were having a great time. So good, in fact, that Electra forgot to check the oven. Suddenly, black smoke rolled out of the huge oven.

"HHHHRRRRRMMM!" Frank roared. "FIRE IS BAD!"

"Don't worry," Electra said. "Burned cookies taste bad but they aren't dangerous." And then Electra gave Frank a hug.

"We have succeeded!" Liza said, clapping her hands.

Just then the man from the mall marched into the snack bar and he didn't look happy.

11

Closed

"I thought there would be a battle over Electra right in the middle of the snack bar," Melody said.

It was the next day and Melody, Liza, Howie, and Eddie were heading back to the ice rink.

"Thank goodness that man took one look at Frank and Electra and realized he might as well pack his bags and leave town," Liza said proudly. "And it's all thanks to me!"

"We helped, too," Howie said. "Especially Eddie."

Eddie stood up tall and puffed out his chest. "I *am* the one who cleared the snack bar in two minutes flat," he bragged.

"I bet Frank and Electra are sitting in a

corner right this minute," Melody said dreamily.

"I hope not," Howie said. "I want a cookie. And not one of those yucky burned ones, either. Even the man in the suit didn't want to eat one."

But when the kids got to the rink they were surprised to find a big sign posted on the snack bar's door. It said CLOSED.

"What happened?" Liza asked. "Where did Electra go?"

"She didn't go anywhere," Eddie said. His nose was pressed flat against the glass door that led into the snack bar. "Electra is right there at the counter. So is Frank."

Liza, Melody, and Howie crowded close to Eddie so they could see. Electra was slumped over the counter, and it looked like she was crying. Frank stood nearby. He didn't look much happier.

"HHHRRRRMMM!" The kids heard Frank groan through the glass. "MY

FAULT!" he roared. "I MAKE OVEN FIRE!"

"Oh no," Liza moaned. "Frank thinks it's his fault that Electra burned those cookies."

"My grandmother burns cookies all the time," Eddie said. "I don't see what the big deal is."

"I don't, either," Howie said, "but I think we better find out."

Howie pushed his friends aside and pulled open the door. Frank and Electra looked up at the kids as they hurried into the snack bar.

"CLOSED!" Frank roared. "NO COOK-IES."

"We didn't come for cookies," Howie said quickly.

Liza nodded. "We're worried about you," she added.

"We don't like to see our friends sad," Melody said. "What's wrong?"

Electra took a shaky breath before explaining. "Mr. Chips hated my cookies," she said with a sob. "All I had left to give him yesterday was the burned batch, and one look at them sent him running."

"Who is Mr. Chips?" Eddie asked.

"The vice president in charge of buying cookies for the Great Flour Cookie Company," Electra explained.

"Oh no," Liza said. "Not *the* famous Great Flour Cookie Company?"

"I know that name," Eddie interrupted. "They sell lots of good cookies."

Electra nodded. "Mr. Chips was interested in marketing my cookies, too. I would have been a cookie executive with my very own company. But now it's too late."

Electra put her head down on the counter and sobbed. Frank patted her on the shoulder, but nothing he did or said could stop her tears.

"Leave now," Frank told the kids. "Must be alone."

Howie, Melody, Liza, and Eddie slowly

left the snack bar and closed the door behind them.

"I feel terrible," Liza said. "I didn't realize that man Electra was with at the mall was Mr. Chips. We ruined Electra's chances of being a successful cookie executive."

"*We* didn't do it," Eddie said. "*You* did."

Liza sighed. "You're right. And it's up to me to fix it."

12

Hauntly Manor Inn

"We have to convince Mr. Chips that Electra's cookies aren't always burned," Liza said, "or Electra's chances of being a cookie executive are ruined."

"What can we do?" Eddie asked.

"It will be simple!" Melody said. "We'll take Mr. Chips a tray of cookies and the cookie problem will be solved."

"A tray of Electra's monster cookies would cost more than an entire week's allowance," Eddie argued.

"You're right," Howie said. "It would take four weeks' worth of allowances."

"Or some of that birthday money Eddie saved," Melody said.

"Wait a minute," Eddie said. "Nobody said anything about donating my birthday money."

Liza grabbed Eddie by the shoulders. "You have to do it," she told him. "Frank's happiness depends on it."

"Besides," Melody said, "he's our friend."

Eddie groaned. "This friendship thing is getting awfully expensive."

"But friendship is worth every penny," Howie said.

Melody, Liza, and Howie waited for Eddie to hurry home and dump his birthday money from his piggy bank. The snack bar was pitch-black when they all got there, and there were no cookies anywhere. "Now what do we do?" Liza moaned.

"Wait a minute," Eddie said, pulling a cookie out of his backpack. "As usual, I have to save the day. I was saving this for later, but I guess it's for a good cause."

Liza jumped up and down. "I could give you a big hug."

Eddie hopped back. "Don't even think about it. Just take this cookie."

The four friends hurried to Hauntly Manor Inn. They stopped when they reached 13 Dedman Street. A chill wind rattled the branches of the dead trees that stood in the yard of the inn.

Hauntly Manor Inn hadn't been open for long but it looked like it was at least three hundred years old. Shutters hung at odd angles and all the windows were etched with jagged cracks. Every kid in Bailey City suspected that Hauntly Manor was haunted.

A black cat perched on the porch stared at Melody, Howie, Liza, and Eddie. Melody gulped. "If we're going to do this, then we better hurry and get it over with," she said.

"You're right," Eddie said before pushing Melody down the broken sidewalk in front of him.

The cat hissed before disappearing into the deep shadows of the backyard. "That's one monster we don't have to worry about," Liza said with a shaky giggle.

Howie took a deep breath before lifting the ancient iron door knocker. He let it fall against the wooden door with a loud thud. The kids heard heavy steps clomping down the hallway. Slowly, the door creaked open.

Melody gasped, Liza whimpered, and Eddie ducked behind Melody. Howie's knees trembled when he looked up at Boris Hauntly.

Boris wore a long black cape buttoned at the throat with a giant clasp that looked exactly like a huge drop of blood. If it wasn't for his red hair, Boris would've been a dead ringer for Dracula.

"Good afternoon," Boris said in his strange Transylvanian accent. When he smiled, the kids couldn't help noticing his two pointy eyeteeth. "Won't you come in?"

"Er . . . no, thank you," Howie stammered. "We just came to see one of your guests."

"His name is Mr. Chips," Melody added.

Boris licked his lips. "Ah, yes," he said. "We have enjoyed his visit. He is packing his suitcase."

"We must see him," Liza blurted, "before he leaves."

"Very well," Boris said. "I will tell him you are here."

Boris disappeared. A few minutes later Mr. Chips appeared at the door. He was the same man they had seen with Electra at the mall. He looked down his nose at the four kids.

"I am a very busy man," he told them. "What do you want?"

"You can't leave," Liza said quickly, "before you have a chance to taste Electra's cookies."

"I have seen them," Mr. Chips said. "They were burnt and nasty."

"Her cookies don't *really* taste like that," Eddie said. "Electra's cookies are the best cookies I've ever tasted."

Howie nodded. "It was our fault they were burned yesterday."

"Here," Liza said, holding Eddie's cookie out to Mr. Chips. "We brought you this to try."

The man looked down at the cookie. "I will take it," he said as he grabbed the cookie, "but I doubt that I'll have time to taste a single bite."

Then Mr. Chips closed the door to Hauntly Manor Inn right in their faces.

13

The Monster Cookie Company

"We were just at the skating rink yesterday," Eddie complained. "Why do we have to go back? I wanted to watch cartoons."

Liza grabbed Eddie's arm and pulled him down Forest Lane. "We have to fix the mess we made yesterday. Howie and Liza are probably already there."

Eddie groaned. All this l-o-v-e business was interfering with his cartoon-watching. And that was pretty serious. He thought about reminding Liza that the whole mess was her fault. He thought about pretending to be sick so he could go home, but he didn't get the chance to do either.

Melody and Howie ran up to them in

front of the Bailey City Ice Skating Complex. "Come quick," Melody shouted. "You'll never believe it!"

"What's the rush?" Eddie said as they raced into the ice rink.

"Look," Howie said as he pointed to the dark snack bar. The only thing that sat on the counter was a crumpled paper cup.

"Look at what?" Eddie asked grumpily. "There's not even one cookie."

"That's what we wanted to show you," Melody said. "Something terrible must have happened. Electra is gone."

Liza slapped her hands to her face. "Oh no!" she cried. "What have I done? I've ruined Electra's life!"

Dr. Victor came up behind the kids and stared at them. "Electra is gone and it's all because of you!"

Liza gulped as Dr. Victor walked closer and closer. Eddie shouted when Dr. Victor grabbed Liza's shoulder. But all Dr. Victor did was pat Liza on the back.

"You mean you're not mad?" Liza asked in a squeaky voice.

Dr. Victor smiled. "Why would I be mad? Electra has never been happier. She told me how you kids gave Mr. Chips your cookie. He loved it."

"It was my cookie," Eddie mumbled.

"Thanks to you," Dr. Victor continued, "Electra is the president of her own company — the Monster Cookie Company."

"Cool!" Melody said, clapping her hands.

Dr. Victor nodded. "Electra has flown to New York to discuss the business deal with the Great Flour Cookie Company and Frank went with her."

Dr. Victor walked away from the kids as Melody moaned. "Oh no. That means New York will be invaded by two monsters."

"Don't worry, New York is used to dealing with monsters," Eddie said.

"It all worked out in the end," Howie said, "so it's good that we helped rid Bai-

ley City of Frankenstein and the Bride of Frankenstein."

Liza sighed and said, "They weren't monsters at all. They were just in *love*."

Eddie groaned and held his stomach. He stopped groaning when Dr. Victor brought them a huge box. "Electra wanted me to give this to you," he explained before he left, "with her thanks."

Eddie tore open the box. It was filled with fifty monster cookies. "Holy Toledo!" Eddie shouted and then he started cramming cookies into his mouth.

Melody laughed and grabbed a cookie. "We may have gotten rid of two monsters," she said, "but there is still one *big* monster left in Bailey City: a cookie monster named Eddie!"

Debbie Dadey and Marcia Thornton Jones have fun writing together. When they both worked at an elementary school in Lexington, Kentucky, Debbie was the school librarian and Marcia was a teacher. During their lunch break in the school cafeteria, they came up with the idea of the Bailey School kids.

Recently Debbie and her family moved to Aurora, Illinois. Marcia and her husband still live in Kentucky where she continues to teach. How do these authors still write together? They talk on the phone and use computers and fax machines!